T0171620

How Thin the Veil

Anne Sports

WESTBOW
PRESS
A DIVISION OF THOMAS NELSON

WestBow Press books may be ordered through booksellers or by contacting:

WestBow Press
A Division of Thomas Nelson
1663 Liberty Drive
Bloomington, IN 47403
www.westbowpress.com
1-(866) 928-1240

ISBN: 978-1-4497-4444-1 (sc)
ISBN: 978-1-4497-4445-8 (e)

Library of Congress Control Number: 2012907254

Printed in the United States of America

WestBow Press rev. date: 8/31/2012

Dedication

For Jesus Christ, whose love makes all things possible; and to my husband, Bert, for the very same reason.

With special thanks to my sister, Jaxn, for her encouragement and expertise.

HOW THIN THE VEIL

IT WAS DARK IN THE chapel. Very dark and very cold. Robin moved slowly down the center aisle, her hand briefly touching the back of each pew she passed, until she reached the final one; the one directly in front of the Reserved Sacrament—the Body of Christ. Robin genuflected and slid onto the bench.

"Hail Mary, full of grace, the Lord is with thee. Blessed art thou amongst women and blessed is the fruit of thy womb, Jesus. Holy Mary, mother of God, pray for us sinners now and at the hour of our death."

Do you walk the halls of this place, Mother Mary? Robin wondered. *Rolling and lifting a walker...rolling and lifting... rolling and lifting? Or are you "damned near scoot-bound" as the old man in apartment 301 complained? Or perhaps you're like my own mother, still new to all this? Too proud to believe you can no longer stand and walk without help, so you simply fall...and fall again.*

Robin sighed. Sobbed. Somehow she knew that this prayer, at least, was heard.

CHAPTER ONE

"The Blessed Virgin rarely appears anymore. It's such a big deal, you know, because of the media. Always turns into a circus." The young man sat down beside Robin. He touched her folded hands. "She asked me to come."

Normally, Robin would have been annoyed. She sought out empty churches for her prayers. She considered other parishioners a distraction, really. However, this young man seemed so painfully shy, so out of place, that she welcomed him. She felt as though she had known him for a very long time; or very long ago; or perhaps in a dream. And yet, words failed her. She smiled and continued her prayers.

"Hail, Holy Queen, Mother of mercy—our life, our sweetness, and our hope. To thee do we cry, poor banished children of Eve—"

"Robin," the stranger whispered, "I am Gabriel."

"The angel?"

"Well, archangel, actually. But yes, the one you're thinking of."

Robin thought this was quite a thing. No sooner had she settled her poor mother into an assisted living facility for patients with dementia than she should lose her own mind. At least she had no qualms about using a walker. She found them rather interesting, really, with all their handy accessories. *Given enough time*, she thought, *man might have evolved into them naturally.*

"I'm honored to make your acquaintance, Archangel," she said steadily.

"You're disappointed, I can tell. Everyone is. They want wings."

But Robin was not disappointed at all. This was her first vision, and she found it fascinating. *How thin the veil between this life and the next.*

Gabriel went on, "I have them, of course. Wings. But they tend to frighten people, and they make sitting difficult. I could show them to you, if you insist."

Robin was smitten by this generous creature. "Not at all," she replied, "though I must say, I hope they're red."

Gabriel grinned. "Red? I would have thought snow white!"

"Once," Robin explained, "I saw a picture of angels with wings of indigo blue, forest green, and gold. But the most beautiful were red."

"Imagine that," said the archangel. "Red!" He smiled to himself.

"Excuse me, sir, but did you say Our Lady sent you?"

"Oh, yes! Yes! As I explained, she avoids showing up herself. Big brou-ha. But as you might imagine, we're very close; ever since the annunciation thing—"

Robin stared in wonder. "I have often pondered that moment. I try to imagine how Mary must have felt. I daresay you showed up fully-winged that time!"

Gabriel blushed. "To be honest, I have a difficult time recalling the details. It's strange—everyone pictures how frightened the Blessed Virgin was, how awe-struck; but *I* was the one entranced. There I was, sent to tell a little child, really, that she was to become a mother!

"And not just any mother—the Theotokos, the God-Bearer...Imagine! A small girl held the fate of mankind! Even now, when she and I speak of it, I tremble. And she just laughs; and her laughter is like the sound of clear water flowing over rocks."

He looked shy again. "Not once did that gentle creature lose heart. That is what she wants me to tell you, Robin. Hold on. You're not alone. (Oh, and get the walker for your mom; and some sensible shoes)."

Robin turned to thank him; but he was gone.

CHAPTER TWO

CHAIR EXERCISE—9 A.M.; REMINISCE WITH Renee—10 a.m.; Macramé: The Art of the Knot—11:30 a.m. Robin glanced at the next day's activities as she poured her second cup of tea. One of the reasons she liked St. Vitus' Village was that it wasn't all Bingo. Some of the facilities they looked at went overboard on the Bingo. It broke her heart to think of women like her mom, who had helped win a war, raised a family, and had successful careers, were now holding buttons and desperately searching for N-36.

But then, Robin's heart broke easily these days. Now she feared her mind was following suit. *Gabriel?!* Still, she had learned not to question anything that brought her comfort. If the truth were told, she felt she needed the peace that her faith provided more than she needed her sanity. Perhaps, she mused, saints are simply lunatics seduced by God. She could live with that.

The telephone startled her out of her reverie. It was an old Bakelite phone; the sort that felt good in your hand. It had some heft, and a deep melodic ring. Robin stroked the receiver lightly. Everything in her old childhood home brought her such pleasure. There was a dear familiarity to it all—a sweet permanence.

"Hello?" she spoke into the receiver.

It was Jack—Jackson—Robin's younger sister, and her closest friend. She had been named after Jack Kennedy. Their mother had been an avid Democrat her entire life until the dementia. It still horrified the girls to hear her spouting conservative views. And the profanity! More and more, their mother's conversation was peppered with words they assumed she was a stranger to.

"Jackson," Robin had informed her sister during her last visit, "your mother just said *Berkeley Hunt*!"

"Wait a minute," Jack responded, scratching her head thoughtfully. "I know this...Berkeley, rhymes-with-Hunt... she never said *that!*"

The sisters (and their inner circle of Anglophile chums) thought it great fun to use "cockney rhyming slang" in place of common vulgarity. The idea is to find a two-word phrase, the second rhyming with the profanity. In theory, you then drop the rhyme, and by using only the innocuous first word, you communicate in glorious, obscene freedom. At least, that's how two bored little sisters felt when they first stumbled across the practice in a dusty tome in their church library. Who knew the section labeled "Anglican Thought" could provide years of ribald entertainment? Robin and Jackson often speculated what daring donor had deposited the waggish book on the shelves. Their parents, meanwhile, had waited patiently, albeit in vain, for the novelty to wear off. *Hampton Wick, Khyber Pass, Raspberry Tart, Ding-dong*

Bell ....Now the dementia had their mother casually using the actual cuss words, not even the innocent rhymes.

Robin had taken her mom's hand, laughing at her stunned sister. "Mom, didn't you say rhymes-with-Berkeley Hunt?"

"Well, yes dear. The television just said a lady spilled hot coffee on her—"

"Berkeley Hunt!" both girls had rejoined, drowning out the offensive rhyme.

Even though the sisters managed to laugh, they knew another bridge had been crossed. They hugged their mother tightly to them, as if that would keep her from drifting any farther.

"Are you there, sis? Should I call back later?" came Jackson's voice in the present, on the phone.

Robin roused herself. "No—sorry. I was just thinking of when mom said Berkeley Hunt."

"Why? You very strange woman!! Of all the things mom ever said—*I'm so proud of you two; you were the loveliest girls at the party; the happiest years of my life were when my daughters were home*—Why do you sit and remember her bellowing *Berkeley Hunt*?!"

"She didn't bellow it," Robin laughed, "and I think about all those other things too. I think about them all the time."

"And so do I," sighed Jackson.

The sisters sat for a few moments in an easy silence, wondering where the years had gone. Growing up in south Louisiana, carried along by the church calendar—Advent, Christmas, Lent, Easter, and the long summer of Pentecost. Watched over by mom and dad, Lydia and Robert Landrey. Their father had died years ago and was buried in a small plot in the private cemetery. Their mother had recently been diagnosed with Alzheimer's. She now lived at St. Vitus Village, an Episcopal assisted living complex. Lydia was safe there. Her daughters hoped she was also happy.

"How is mom?" Jackson finally asked.

"I'm going to visit her after breakfast," Robin replied. "Today they're making Belgian waffles; you know how she looks forward to those."

Jackson knew. "We'll have to start watching her weight, I'm afraid. She hates all the exercise classes."

"Except the walking club," Robin corrected her, "but she still refuses to attend water aerobics. She told me she can't stand seeing all those wrinkled old people!"

They both burst out laughing.

"But SHE'S a wrinkled, old person!"

"I know," sighed Robin, "but I guess she doesn't see it."

"Anyway…how are you coping?" Jackson asked.

Robin considered lying; but why? If anyone could understand, it would be Jack. Both girls had been raised in a devoutly orthodox household; baptized and confirmed in the Episcopal faith. Their brand of Anglo-Catholic piety was the norm in south Louisiana. Robin and Jackson grew up under the loving gaze of Jesus, with His Sacred Heart, and Mary, with her Immaculate one.

"I was a little down yesterday," Robin replied, "but Our Lady sent Gabriel with a few words of encouragement; so, you know, that helped."

"Idiot!" Jackson guffawed.

"And with thy spirit. How are you and Sam?"

"Busy. He's got a show this weekend. He's in the shop, designing presentation boxes for the pens. I'm working on a new font for the engraving…but if you need me…" Jack always offered to drop everything and make the trip from Houston to Fairhope; and Robin knew she was sincere.

They had spent weeks together, sorting things out. Deciding what to do when it became apparent that Lydia could no longer live alone. Robin had finally moved back from Baton Rouge. There was really nothing keeping her there, since the death of her husband the previous year.

Perhaps, she mused, grief had unhinged her mind. First her beloved Will's death; now her mother's illness. She was beginning to feel hexed. *It won't do any harm*, she thought, *to give the heavenly host a chance before resorting to a gris-gris bag.* Like most things in Louisiana, religion was an appealing gumbo of exotic ingredients. Things mysterious were not just accepted, they were celebrated. Normally with a parade and masked ball. Her father once told her, laughing, that in Louisiana, the only truly unpardonable sin was being boring. It is a miraculous place, altogether.

"Sis?" Jack was still on the line; "Shall I come for a while?"

Robin smiled. "Nah; I'm fine. WE'RE fine. I'm heading for the village right now."

"Give mom my love, okay?" Jackson smiled, "Oh, and Gabriel, too!"

Robin hung up the phone, chuckling. If she hurried, she could stop by the chapel before joining Lydia.

CHAPTER THREE

"Jackson sends her regards."

Robin's return to the chapel had found her new friend Gabriel already there.

He grinned at her greeting. "What a lovely child! Always has been. Her patron, C.S. Lewis, calls her a sparkler, you know. 'Just praying for my little sparkler,' he'll say."

"I'll let her know," Robin assured him. "She'll be so pleased! We adore our patron saints, of course. Can you tell me about mine?"

"Let's see...July 12th," the archangel considered, "that would be Veronica, I believe. Wonderful woman. A special favorite of the Blessed Virgin; rushing out to help her fallen Son and all. But you'll meet her soon, my dear. You can draw your own conclusions. Do give Jackson my best, however. Delightful creature."

Robin agreed with Gabriel's assessment. Everyone did. People were immediately drawn to her younger sister. She had a knack for making them feel they had her undivided attention. They basked in her genuine interest in them.

Jackson was petit and blonde, with emerald eyes and a winning smile; intelligent, amusing, and unfailingly kind. She was, in all honesty, everything Robin would have liked to be.

Robin, on the other hand, was tall and thin; all elbows and knees. A nondescript brunette with angular features. She did, at least, boast beautiful eyes—the color of Dawn dish liquid.

Robin was utterly amazed at Jack's ability to put people at ease. She found it easier to withdraw; preferring solitude to crowds, silence to noise, and darkness to the harsh glare of daylight.

Despite their differences, the sisters were devoted to one another, and, almost since birth, to God (whom they defined simply as *Love*).

Their lives, like their personalities, were also completely different—yet they suited each girl. Robin had married the month after completing high school; a young boy she had met at church. She and Will moved to Baton Rouge, where he worked at the tiny airport. Robin worked part-time at various odd jobs. They were happy and in love; it never occurred to them to ask for more.

Jackson viewed life as an adventure. She traveled the world, making friends and taking lovers. She'd send Robin letters from distant lands, telling of exotic scenes and fascinating men. Robin would write back, talking of happy holidays and romantic wedding anniversaries and dear neighbors. Each of them was content with her own life—and happy for the other.

Jack eventually met a man who captured her roving heart (along with her extensive wardrobe of Victoria's Secret power lingerie, much to his delight). They met, as you might imagine, on a beach in the Caribbean and were married on a pirate ship in Las Vegas. They had made their home in Houston.

The one common thread in the two sisters' lives, apart from their faith, was their inability to have children. Tumors, tilted uterus, a missing ovary. "Don't ask! I'm as barren as the accursed fig tree!" It grieved Jackson more than Robin. She viewed motherhood as the ultimate adventure. To Robin, it was one fraught with peril. A sensitive child herself, she knew how easily a little one could be hurt.

"It's all about fear, isn't it, my darling?" a gentle voice inquired, drawing Robin back to the present. "It can be paralyzing. I remember how the entire world seemed frozen." But there was nothing but warmth in her smile now.

Robin looked up, trying to focus through her tears. She managed to whisper, "Veronica?"

CHAPTER FOUR

"At last we meet, face to face," said the soft-spoken saint. "Of course, I've known you since the day you were born. July 12—my feast day!" She was lovely, with an inner beauty that shown in her face.

"Thank you for all your prayers, my lady," said Robin, sincerely.

"Please, call me Veronica—it means *True Image*, you know, because of my veil and all. Even so, I like to think I reflect a bit of His love in my very self! And you're welcome, for the prayers."

Robin was mesmerized. "For your example, as well. I try so hard to have not only your compassion, but your courage, too."

Veronica is commemorated in the Stations of the Cross. Taking pity on Christ as He was being led to Calvary, she broke through the jeering crowd and wiped His battered face with her veil. Miraculously, His image was imprinted there. Robin wore the saint's medal, along with a small crucifix, around her neck always.

"You've thought of me quite often, I know." Veronica seemed touched by this. "One Lent, as I recall, you prayed to be allowed to see what I saw, when I stooped, to wipe His face."

"That's right! I asked to gaze into Jesus' eyes, as He struggled to the place of crucifixion. It sounds so presumptuous, doesn't it?" Robin knew she was blushing.

Veronica placed her hands on either side of Robin's face. "Dear one," she whispered, "why would such a sweet request be presumptuous? Now let me tell you what you would have seen. Indeed, what I saw: your own reflection. Concern for you and for me filled His eyes and His heart. You would have seen yourself, for that is all He saw."

Robin was stunned by this simple truth. Like an old friend, she had sat many an hour with Christ and felt the concern that her patron spoke of. Concern for her grief, her pain, her confusion; and somehow the knowledge of that constant care kept her from complete despair.

"And here is another mystery," Veronica continued, "your heart bears His image as surely as my veil does."

Robin was filled with wonder. She groped for words. "Thank you...thank you for coming. It's going to be all right, isn't it? I mean, my mom and everything—"

Veronica nodded her head, smiling broadly. "I have a dear friend, Julian. Such a wise, talented soul. She always says, 'And all things shall be well; and all things shall be well; and all manner of things shall be well!' We're both praying for you. Now, you'd better run along; Community Crossword is starting!"

She blew a kiss and vanished.

CHAPTER FIVE

As it turned out, there was no need to hurry. For some reason, only a handful of residents were gathered around the large table in the activities center. Normally, every chair was taken and extras had to be brought in from the dining room. It was a popular pastime—filling in the oversized crossword puzzle, sitting on an easel at the front of the room. Complimentary Krispy Kreme doughnuts were an added enticement. Surprisingly, Robin was able to slip into the chair next to her mother, proudly clutching her favorite, a jelly-filled.

"Good morning, moms! How were the waffles?" She kissed her mother and hugged her firmly.

"I missed them. I overslept," she yawned.

"Oh, I'm sorry. Would you like a doughnut?" Robin offered.

"Chocolate!" Lydia demanded. Robin marveled how her mother seemed more and more like a child. What a strange disease, dementia. Alzheimer's. She brought her the pastry and a napkin. "Jackson sends her love—"

"Shhh! They're starting!"

Renee, the bubbly Activities Director at St. Vitus Village, began the puzzle, as she did everything, beaming at the assembled residents. She read the clues like a town crier and marked the correct answers in the squares with a flourish.

"A dark wood—five letters—begins with an E. Jim?" Wheelchair Jim always sat at the head of the table; he had to maneuver into place. Lydia considered him a totally unpleasant man. "He smokes like a chimney and throws up on his balcony," she confided. No further explanation was forthcoming. The girls had learned not to ask too many questions.

"*Ebony*!" Wheelchair barked.

"Right, Jim! Next: a rough file—four letters—begins with an R. This is a hard one, Geraldine."

Gerry consulted with her roommate, Annie. Robin and Jackson were convinced these two were lesbians, much to their amusement. They had taken to humming "The Look of Love" whenever their mother mentioned them.

"Is it a *rasp*?" Geraldine guessed. It was.

Lydia's new best friend, Miriam, slightly embarrassed herself by guessing that "A Legendary Himalayan" was Yoda; but Renee seamlessly inked in *Yeti*. Miriam had been placed in St. Vitus by her husband, a much younger man, who subsequently filed for divorce. Lydia sighed, "She cries a lot. I suggested she talk to the priest. But she's Jewish."

Hugh, the Vietnam vet and would-be Casanova, had dozed off and missed his turn. Lydia correctly guessed his word and her own, to Robin's secret delight. Then Lydia, too, began to nod.

"Mom, why is everyone so tired?"

"Some of them are still in bed, actually. We all stayed up too late."

Robin wasn't sure she liked the sound of this. The latest thing on yesterday's calendar was "Poker—2:30."

"Doing what?: she whispered.

"There was the loveliest wedding, dear. By candlelight!" Lydia smiled, dreamily.

"But where? Was it a movie?"

"No…of course not…what movie?" Lydia looked confused. "It was a wedding. In the chapel, of course. Just a small one, but so nice…all the candles—oh, it's my turn!"

Renee was waiting. "A soap component—three letters—ends in an E."

"*Lye*, I think," Lydia resumed, "now please let me concentrate! This isn't easy!"

"But the wedding…" Robin prompted.

"What wedding? I'll need a new hat if we're going to a wedding. Are there any more doughnuts?"

Robin wiped the chocolate from her mother's chin and went for another Krispy Kreme. "Damn!" Someone had snagged the last of the jellies.

By the time the crossword puzzle was complete, a few more of Lydia's neighbors had drifted down. There was Ellery, dapper as always in his bowtie; he was the star of the St. Vitus' dance classes. And strange Edna. Jackson was certain she was a virgin (or if she had sex, Robin wagered, it was with one of her many cats). Jigsaw Jane had taken her seat at the card table and was busy working on a 1,000-piece picture of Pug dogs.

Robin often wondered what she would say about her own self, if she walked into the village. "Robin, the delusional old widow who hoards jelly doughnuts." Now she could add, "and is visited by various saints and martyrs." She'd fit right in! If I could just start throwing up on my balcony, she mused.

Of course, there were many perfectly nice, but perfectly non-descript, folk at St. Vitus. Lydia was a member of this group. Pleasant people whose only peculiarity was a malfunction deep in their brains that robbed them of their past and future, leaving them in the eternal present. A clock—or calendar—confused Lydia utterly. The present moment was all she had.

CHAPTER SIX

IT BEING WEDNESDAY, THERE WAS Walking Club after Community Crossword. The little group made a circuit around the complex, picking their way slowly and carefully along, chatting. Lately, Lydia had begun falling. Sometimes tripping, sometimes losing her balance, sometimes simply collapsing. The sisters had encouraged her to use a walker or, at least, a cane. So far, she had refused to even consider it. They feared one of her falls would result in an injury that would not heal.

Robin left Lydia to her walking (and subsequent "Pedicure—11 a.m." and "Watercolors—1:30"). She would return at 3:00 to attend Mass with her. Father David George celebrated Holy Eucharist in the St. Vitus chapel every Wednesday, afternoon, rain or shine.

Father George was the rector at All Souls Episcopal Church in Fairhope. Robin had known him virtually all of her life. He had prepared her for Confirmation, heard her first Confession, and performed the wedding ceremony for her and Will.

During her father's final illness and subsequent death, she had spent many happy hours with this kindly priest, discussing any number of topics related to the church, fortifying herself with a glass of whiskey. Without exception, their talks always concluded with Father George reminding her, "It's all about love, little one."

Robin considered All Souls extremely fortunate to be shepherded by such a loving and orthodox priest. The Episcopal Church, like all denominations, was undergoing its share of change. It was a shock to discover that most parishes in Baton Rouge had followed the post-Vatican II trend and jettisoned all that was beautiful and thought-provoking. Simply finding a church with an altar, rather than a free-standing communion table, became the start of a scavenger hunt for the newlyweds. *Altar? Check! Holy Water? Check! Sanctus Bell? Check! Rosary? Damn! Skunked again!* Still, Robin and Will clung steadfastly to the Anglo-Catholic "high church" piety as taught them by dear, black-cassocked Fr. George.

Returning to Fairhope and All Souls was a balm to Robin's spirit, in that respect. She could once again hail Mary to her heart's content. And did.

And so, 3:15 found her kneeling at the altar rail, "tongue extended over lower teeth," as per the catechism, receiving the Host. Her mother, preferring the contemporary method, gazed lovingly into her palms. "The Body of Our Lord Jesus Christ," Father George proclaimed. Surely, Robin hoped, even dementia could not diminish the power of such profound love.

Robin spoke to her mom briefly, at the end of the service. "Will I see you tomorrow, then?"

"Oh, no, dear! Not tomorrow! I forgot to tell you, we're taking the bus up the highway to the outlet mall!" Lydia burbled excitedly. "I need to go shopping!"

"For what, mom? I could pick things up for you." She steadied her mother, on the chapel steps.

"But I need to try things on," Lydia explained. "I'm looking for a dressy outfit. But festive. And I'd like a hat!"

"Goodness!" Robin laughed. "Must be quite an occasion! I'll have to check your calendar."

Lydia explained, off-handedly, "Oh, I'm sure it won't be on the calendar. There's to be another wedding. And," she confided, lowering her voice, "rumor has it, this one is going to be a formal affair!"

CHAPTER SEVEN

Robin stared as her mother hurried away (the van to the library departed at 4).

She turned and re-entered the chapel, hoping Father George would still be there. Sure enough, he was clearing the altar and replacing the flower arrangements.

"Aren't they especially beautiful this week?" Robin commented.

"Yes, indeed," Father agreed. "All white has always seemed so very elegant to me." He gently cupped a Calla Lilly.

"Of course! They're from last night's wedding!" Robin laughed. "Mom swears she attended a ceremony!"

A bemused expression passed over the old priest's face. "They do get rather strange ideas, don't they?"

The two friends sat together in the first pew. "I suppose she was dreaming," Robin speculated.

"Then at least it was a lovely dream—attending a wedding. Do you know, I can still recall every detail of yours, my sweet? You wore white, of course, and Jackson wore red, for a Christmas wedding. William had cut himself shaving and had a small piece of sticking-plaster on his chin!"

"That's right!" Robin laughed. "It's there in all the pictures. He was mortified!"

"You miss him very much, don't you?" Father George took her hand and stroked it gently.

Robin thought for a moment. "When Will first died, the pain was so...acute. I wondered if I could stand it. Now, it is a constant, dull ache that never goes away. I carry the knowledge of what I have lost like some terrible weight." She looked away, embarrassed.

"That is called coping, I believe. Learning to carry the weight, and not be crushed by it."

"Oh, Father, I have missed our talks!" Robin confided, gratefully.

"As have I," the priest agreed; and she knew he meant it. "Let me see," he considered, "if I remember correctly—which I invariably do (on this subject, at any rate)—you always appreciated a single-malt Scotch."

Robin blushed. "Too true!"

"Then please, will you come and see me at the vicarage? We can discuss whatever you'd like—our mutual love of Tolkien, our mutual loathing of 'electric praise bands,' even these phantom weddings, if you'd like," Father George chuckled. "Will you come?"

Robin felt better already. "Yes, thank you. I'd love to. But..."

"Oh, dear! You're not an alcoholic are you?! I'd hate to think I started you down *that* road—" the priest looked startled.

"No, no!" Robin reassured him, "The truth is, I do need to speak to you about something that's been, well, troubling me. A bit. Oh, Father, it's no big deal, really...I've been seeing saints!...There! That's it!"

Father George covered his mouth with his hand. Robin thought for a moment that he was hiding a smile.

"Saints?" he asked.

"Yes. And angels."

"Here? In the chapel, I mean?" he further inquired.

How curious, Robin thought. Perhaps he doesn't understand. She tried again. "Father, I see saints, and they talk to me. And I wonder what it means and what I should do and if—"

The priest once again took Robin's hand in his; he gazed intently into her blue eyes; and he whispered, "You are not going mad. But before you rally the troops and defend the Dauphine against the British, my little Joan of Arc, come to the vicarage and talk to me. Tomorrow, at our usual time?" He remembered too, then, their regular schedule back in those difficult days?

"I'll come," she said, bemused.

"Good. In the meantime, I wouldn't worry about seeing saints. Some people would think it's better than seeing, say, Wheelchair Jim." With that, he rose, genuflected to the altar, and walked out of the chapel.

CHAPTER EIGHT

"I DO WISH YOU'D EXPLAIN one thing to me," Gabriel was standing beside her, watching Father George sweep past. "There you have a tremendous saint of the church, who you're not at all startled to encounter; but let Padre Pio visit, and you think you're losing your grip on sanity!"

"I suppose," said Robin. "It's the death thing."

"The death thing!" laughed the archangel. "You mortals make too much of a trifle."

"I think I agree with you there," sighed Robin. "Mom's Alzheimer's has taught me…well, that there are worse fates than dying. Now I only ask for mercy. Anyway, I'm glad to see you again," she added quietly.

"Thank you! I was hoping you didn't find my popping in and out, well, off-putting."

"Not at all," she assured him. "Tell me—can Father George see you? He didn't seem a bit shocked when I told him about…things."

"He can see me, yes. And sometimes he does. You see, angels only appear when they are sent." Gabriel sat down and settled into the pew.

"And saints?" prompted Robin.

"Ah, saints. They appear when they are needed."

Robin considered this. "Gabriel, are the saints needed *here*, in this chapel? But why?"

Gabriel beamed. "Yes, dear girl! That's exactly it! We are all needed in this humble chapel. To fill it with love and joy and to bear witness—." He stopped, surprised at his own emotion. "But that is not my story to tell. Your Father George will explain everything." He stood and gazed about the empty chapel.

"Are you leaving?" Robin was suddenly feeling very melancholy.

"I must. As I say, angels are sent. I'm looking for darling Saint Francis, at the moment. He set out to speak with you over a week ago, in your time. He often becomes distracted by...oh, a deer, or a dog, or even a beautiful rose bush in bloom. He can sit for days on end, marveling at the slow determination of a turtle and giving thanks to the Creator. A charming man; but a handful!"

"He's Lydia's patron!" Robin informed the angel.

"Of course. I've seen the statue on her front porch." Gabriel chuckled to himself. "The other day, I overheard Francis asking Stephen (the patron of stone-masons, you see) why he was never portrayed with a walking frame. He felt it might make your mother less self-conscious if she saw him on one! He looked so sincere, poor Stephen actually promised to look into it! Such a lovely child, that Francis. Never had an unkind thought."

"I hope you find him," offered Robin.

"He'll turn up," Gabriel assured her. "In the meantime, I'll leave you here with our Lord." He bowed to the altar and brushed the tabernacle with his lips. "Hail, True Body," the two whispered together. And the archangel was gone.

Robin knelt reverently before the Reserved Sacrament. *Strange*, she thought, *though Christ has never appeared to me and only speaks within my own spirit, I've always felt closer to Him than anyone else. Living or dead, as it turns out.*

The hours of the afternoon slipped away in utter contentment, as they always do when dear friends meet.

CHAPTER NINE

Robin finished her prayers just in time to see two men enter the chapel.

"I found him!" announced the older of the two. He was a thin man, bronzed by the sun, grinning widely. "He was poking around the garden, weren't you, Francis?" He was obviously very fond of the little friar who followed him in, glancing shyly at Robin.

The elder saint extended his hand. "And you must be Robin! I'm Fiacre, and very pleased to make your acquaintance!"

Robin rose and exclaimed excitedly, "Patron of gardeners, I believe! The pleasure is mine, sir. My late husband had a statue of you among his herbs."

"So he did!" Fiacre seemed happy to be recognized. "My friend needs no introduction, I'm sure. Robin, may I present Saint Francis of Assisi."

Francis had been strolling by The Stations of the Cross, tenderly touching each one. When he heard his name, he glanced quizzically at Fiacre, then at Robin, and finally turned back to the stations.

"Don't mind him," Fiacre whispered. "He hates being noticed. Introductions are especially hard on him, poor lad." He raised his voice, "We've been having a lovely time in the garden, haven't we, Francis? Such a splendid bounty this time of year!"

Francis made his way to sit near his friend. He smiled and patted the pew, inviting Robin to be seated. She noticed his palms were wound with strips of cloth, and wondered. Francis quickly tucked them into his cloak.

Fiacre continued, winking, "It takes a bit of time to tour a garden with Francis, I must say. We have to keep pausing to thank our friends—Brother Sun, Sister Rain, Brother Wind, Sister Shade, Brother Earthworm, Sister Soil, Brother Bee—." He laughed heartily.

"Tell your mother that people think I'm demented, too," Francis spoke for the first time, not minding Fiacre's gentle teasing.

"Then people are wrong! "Fiacre rejoined, emphatically. "Personally, I think you see things more clearly than most. *You* see our Lord in all His creation. It's a wonderful gift."

Saint Francis blushed and fingered his coarse robe. "And," he continued, "remind her, please, that I'm praying for her; especially now. It is tedious to grow old and to feel one's body wearing out." He paused, considering a moment, and added, "She will be renewed, in God's time, as all things are." He glanced at Robin, to be sure she understood.

"I…thank you, Francis. I'm so touched that you came."

"I'm Lydia's patron," the saint replied. "It is my care and delight."

He looked relieved that his mission had ended. At least the verbal part. He rose and walked silently to the altar. There he dropped to his knees and lifted his eyes in adoration. His face radiated contentment; an aura of familiar recognition seemed to pass between the saint and the Sacrament.

"He's quite a wonder, isn't he?" Fiacre asked, as if reading Robin's thoughts.

"Indeed he is. I wish I had been more… at ease. I found myself utterly tongue-tied," Robin sighed quietly.

"Everyone feels that way around Francis, of course. But rest assured, it was his wish to visit you. When he heard that a few of us had noticed your trips to the chapel, he offered to pitch in. 'An instrument of thy peace' and all that!" Fiacre winked again.

Robin smiled through her tears. "Thank you, too, Saint Fiacre. I can't say that I understand any of this; but my heart grows lighter when I'm in this place."

"One day soon," Fiacre promised, glancing around the chapel, "you'll begin to understand that these pews are filled with love and hope and tolerance. That is really the message we all bring."

"When, Fiacre?"

"Perhaps at the next wedding!" the saint chuckled. "Come, Francis, we must be going. Gabriel is searching high and low for you, you scamp!"

"Actually," Fiacre confided in Robin, as Francis made his way to the back of the church, "our Lord Himself loves having Francis close to Him; He misses him terribly when he strays the least little bit. Two of a kind, they are. Deep calling to deep."

Fiacre hugged Robin and bid her farewell. Francis turned and waved his bandaged hand. As if in blessing, he announced, "How happy are the merciful! For they shall have nothing but mercy shown to them!"

Arm in arm, the companions departed.

CHAPTER TEN

THE FOLLOWING DAY FOUND LYDIA with a bus-load of residents on the way to the outlet stores, in search of high fashion at low prices. Robin just hoped the same number of neighbors got off the bus as had got on. Along with their purses and purchases. With dementia, everything became an adventure.

Robin herself took the opportunity to resume her visits with Father George. She wondered if the vicarage had changed over the years. Would her favorite over-stuffed loveseat still be there, opposite Father's leather chair? Would the official portraits of the Queen and the Archbishop of Canterbury still smile down on her from over the fireplace? One thing she knew for certain—books would be everywhere. In cases, atop tables, stacked on the floor...Father George once remarked that he pictured paradise as a vast library. Tomes stacked floor to ceiling; with one of those rolling ladders at his disposal. She often thought Father George loved books the way some men love women. Everything about them brought him pleasure. He was happiest at home, in the midst of his own harem. The sultan's favorite, of course, was the Holy Bible. Followed closely by the 1928 Book of Common Prayer (though he had capitulated to the more recent version. Rite One, exclusively. "Our island home! What rubbish!" he'd storm, sending Robin into fits of giggling). He really is an old crank, Robin surmised; in all things except love. That, he spreads lavishly and indiscriminately. It was this compassion that made him a darling man and a perfect priest to his parishioners.

As she made her way up the path to the priest's home, the door swung open. "Prompt, as always!" Father George saluted her.

"I'm afraid I'm one of those insufferable people who is always on time for appointments," responded Robin.

"Not at all," the priest admonished. "It shows consideration for others."

"In my case, it shows a lack of anything to fill my time," Robin confessed.

"Leisure is no sin, my dear. Come in, at any rate; you're always welcome."

She needn't have worried about time altering the pastor's home. She sighed as she settled into the loveseat, tucking her feet up under her.

"It's all just as I remember," Robin told him, happily.

Father George pretended an attempt at straightening the clutter. "Your wonderful sister took a series of photos featuring my books, did you know? She shelved them with odd bits of pottery, and stacked them in various places, and tossed them about, artfully—she's awfully good."

Jackson was a professional photographer. She had done a series of scenes—the priest's library, the statuary in the church cemetery, and the architectural details of All Souls itself. The ladies guild had converted them into greetings cards as a parish fundraiser.

The priest continued, "The cards were gorgeous. Huge success. And what a treat, having Jack around. She lit up the place."

Robin smiled. "C.S. Lewis says she's a sparkler."

Father George paused, staring into her eyes. "I think," he finally said, "that is my cue to pour the Scotch."

He reached into a deep desk drawer and took out a bottle and two tumblers.

Robin cried in amazement, "The Mac Allan! You remembered!" It was her favorite distillery.

The priest shrugged, but was obviously pleased. "When I'm defrocked, I can always obtain a position tending bar."

"The two professions have much in common, I've always thought," teased Robin. "Hearing confessions, giving advice, offering consolation..."

"I daresay the wage would be an improvement." Father George handed her a glass and lifted his own. "To the Communion of Saints!" he toasted.

"Amen!" Robin responded; then added, "To the Great Cloud of Witnesses!"

"Amen, indeed!"

Both of them knew that it was time for a talk. Father George began.

CHAPTER ELEVEN

"Robin, do you remember Eva Bordelon? Long-time member of the parish? Sweet woman. Played the organ for the sung services."

Robin thought back to her days at All Souls. "I think so. Rather large woman...unusual taste in jewelry."

"Lord, yes! Huge necklaces—looked like something from The Flintstones!" Father George smiled. "Bless her, she was one of the first to move into St. Vitus. Ended up living there for over 10 years. Her only visitors in all that time were her son, Troy, and his partner, Dean. Two of the dearest people I've ever met."

Robin interrupted, "Do you mean business partner or...?"

"I mean Troy and Dean were gay. They were lovers."

"Hmmm," Robin sipped her drink.

"Yes, hmmm. Towards the end of Eva's life (may she rest in peace)," he crossed himself, "she began giving Dean gifts. Beautiful things that she had obviously kept stored for years. Lace tablecloths, embroidered pillow-cases, sterling picture frames and dresser sets…I don't know what all. The boys were baffled; but they had learned over the years not to make too much of Eva's behavior." The priest paused in his narrative. "Another drink?" he offered.

"No, thanks. I'm fine." Robin stretched on the loveseat, willing him to continue.

"Then one day, Eva brought out a small chest, telling Dean she wanted him to have the contents. Inside, carefully packed in tissue paper, were Troy's baby clothes. His christening gown and first communion suit, a tiny cowboy outfit, several hand-made booties and lace bibs. It finally occurred to them that she thought the lads were married. Troy tried to explain that he and Dean loved each other very much; he assured her that all the presents were lovely, but that she didn't have to part with them. That is when she said, 'But Troy, I've been saving them all these years to give to the person you married. Dean is your wife, isn't he?' He told me Eva looked so confused—and utterly crestfallen. The boys came to see me the next day. They asked if I would bless their union. Perform some simple ceremony."

"Had they known each other long?" Robin queried.

Father George laughed, "Didn't I say? They'd been together for 32 years!" He refreshed their drinks.

"What did you do?"

"I prayed," he chuckled. "I asked Troy and Dean to let me consider things. I knew the bishop wouldn't allow any official ceremony at All Souls. There *isn't* any official ceremony sanctioned by the church, to begin with. Perhaps, I thought, I could simply bless these two men, living in love—hell, I bless pets, and homes, and Rosary beads! But what were the theological implications? And did I want to get into all this? What if word got out? I'm an old man, Robin; I'll be retiring one of these days. I'd like to leave my vocation in good standing; and with my income intact, God forgive me. On the other hand, all they wanted was to make a confused old woman happy, by being happy themselves. They wanted to give her the family she'd been waiting for; she had so little time left. Back and forth I went, until I was exhausted. And I still had no answers."

"Poor dear Father." Robin could hear the anguish in his voice. "Who does a priest go to for counsel?"

Father smiled at her question. "You know the answer to that, I'm sure—The High Priest, of course." He sipped his whiskey. "I was on my way to visit Eva, knowing Troy and Dean would expect an answer. I stopped by the chapel and knelt before the altar." His eyes were searching hers, ready to stop his tale if he saw any sign of retreat; but her gaze was steady. She knew what was coming.

"He was an imposing figure. Solid. His voice, though halting, was soft and warm. He introduced himself—Thomas of Aquino. Thomas Aquinas. The greatest theologian and philosopher in all Christendom. I was awe-struck. Dumb-founded. And immensely grateful. I begged him to tell me what to do."

Father George had picked up a large volume from a set of handsomely bound books. Robin recognized it as one of the priest's prized possessions—*The Summa Theologica*, by Saint Thomas.

Father George continued his narrative. "The saint touched the red lamp above the Reserved Sacrament, setting it gently swinging. Whenever I was wrestling with a difficult question and felt I had reached an impasse," he told me, "I would rest my head on the tabernacle where our dear Lord resides. In time, the answer always became clear. Ah, Aquinas! He is more than brilliant, Robin. He is enlightened."

Robin longed to ask more, much more. She was sure they had spoken at length. She wanted details! But she instinctively knew that these facts were not for her. What passed between the two men belonged to Father George alone. And she rejoiced with him.

"So," the priest declared, joyfully, "there I was! Where I should have been all along. When you have questions about love, go to the source!"

"And what was His answer?"

"As I waited there in the silence, I recalled the words of Saint Paul: 'And I will show you a still more excellent way.' It's the line he writes to the people of Corinth, just before he tells them about the nature of love—"

"In Chapter 13!" Robin interjected.

"You make an old priest very proud!" He filled their glasses again. "And very thirsty."

"So you blessed Troy and Dean, I assume?" Robin asked, sipping contentedly.

"You assume correctly. In the chapel at St. Vitus. Frail, sweet Eva was so pleased. It was a very quick, simple service. I read the chapter you mentioned; bound Troy and Dean's hands together; and blessed them, "In nomine Patris, et Filii, et Spiritus Sancti."

"Nice touch—the Latin!" laughed Robin.

"Oh, the gay Anglo-Catholics love it!" Father George joined in the laughter, good-naturedly.

"So, was it just the four of you, that first time?"

"Yes…and no," the priest's eyes twinkled. And Robin's grew very big indeed.

"The saints?" she whispered.

Father George nodded. "Saint Thomas knew I needed… support. Confirmation, perhaps. My dear, I'm a company man; I don't break ranks on a regular basis. But this—this Love—is worth risking everything for! I so longed for a joyful, not a furtive, occasion."

"And did you get it?" But she knew the answer.

"Good heavens, what a wonderful sight! Aquinas, of course. And Saint Valentine, naturally. Francis and Clair. Your Veronica and my George (sans dragon, thankfully), with Bede and Augustine of Canterbury (the English made a good showing); oh, and Vitus and some fearful angels—." He was beaming.

"You alone could see them?"

"Yes, of course. And these days, the residents have discovered the services; so the blessed saints no longer attend as often. The old darlings have really taken to the ceremonies; and the couples seem to bask in their acceptance."

"But that's wonderful, Father."

"As far as it goes. But it's essential that it remain a "non-event," as they say. It cannot become an issue in the parish. And any mention of the saints would be sheer madness." The strain showed in the dear priest's face. But he mastered it and grinned. "We walk by faith, dear friend."

Robin agreed. But she wasn't sure she'd be able to walk at all if she had any more of the Mac Allan.

Father George, on the other hand, had been pacing quite steadily for the last 15 minutes. At last, he sank into his worn leather chair.

"There you have it. Well, most of it. Believe it or not, that is the first time I've related the entire story."

He chuckled, "That is one of the benefits of going batty at a memory-care facility! No one takes anything that you say or do very seriously." The priest reached for his glass.

"And if they do," Robin added, "the next day it's all forgotten."

"Welcome to bedlam!" was his final toast.

CHAPTER TWELVE

FATHER GEORGE AND ROBIN SAT in relaxed silence, lost in their own thoughts. Finally, the priest joined her on the loveseat, patting her socked feet.

"There are more things in heaven and earth, Horatio, than are dreamt of in your philosophy," he offered.

Robin was convinced of it. "So, Father," she murmured as she considered his words.

"Hmmm?" he raised his eyebrows.

"Is St. Vitus becoming a wedding destination? Like Las Vegas? Or worse—Gatlinburg?!"

"But without the corn-cob pipes and jugs of moonshine?!" he guffawed. "Perish the thought! First of all, these aren't weddings. Holy matrimony is a sacrament that, for good or ill, is denied to same-sex couples. I give a simple blessing to those who seek it. In a simple ceremony. Since Dean and Troy, which was four years ago, I've performed less than 10. It's a very small part of my ministry."

"Do relatives attend?" Robin was bursting, with questions, much to Father George's amusement.

"Rarely. Perhaps that's why the couples don't mind the residents. They stand in for their families, I suppose," he considered.

"Is there a reception?"

"Never has been. It is, as I say, kept very low-key. The couples who contact me are seeking something spiritual. They need to know that they, and their love, are acceptable. They don't want a party."

"Or they'd go to Gatlinburg?" Robin grinned, "for a hillbilly jamboree!"

"Not on your life! These are gay men!" the priest laughed. "It's all very tasteful."

"You've not blessed women? I mean lesbians?"

"Only once." He considered before answering. "Geraldine and Annie."

Robin's jaw dropped. "You did not!"

"Didn't really have much choice", Father George chuckled. "Once they realized what was going on, those two became regular attendees. Finally, they cornered me. Annie barked, 'See here! We have sat side-by-side in the pew at All Souls for more than 43 years, listening to you paraphrase *Crystal Blue Persuasion*'…"

Robin laughed hysterically as her priest, in his pleasant tenor voice, sang, "Love is the answer to every equation." She joined in, providing the back-up vocals.

"Basically," he concluded, "they were asking me the same question I had been asking myself. Did I believe it or not? We held the service the following evening."

Robin would have given anything to have been there.

"It's not a ceremony I'm likely to forget," Father told her. "It was very sweet, of course. Geraldine looked just radiant.

At the conclusion, Annie burst into an impromptu version of *Because God Made You Mine* that can only be described as stunning. Saint Cicilia had a suspicious coughing fit and had to make a hasty exit! What a night!"

Robin could picture it all. She had only one more question. "When is the next service?"

To her surprise, Father George sighed loudly. He explained that he had, indeed, been contacted by a gay couple, Philip and Johnathon.

"It's a matter of John making the trip from their home in Atlanta. He's very ill. First the flight, then a rental car, and all in one day. Well, Philip is working on the details."

"If there is anything I can do," Robin offered, "just let me know. Really."

The priest seemed to appreciate her offer. But apparently he thought there was something more she had to understand.

"It's not simply a matter of an overnight stay, I'm afraid. John is in the final stages of AIDS. I believe it's one reason that they want so badly to receive this blessing. To remember their love as a holy thing. To be surrounded by tenderness, at the end. Would you be willing to be a part of all that, if it meant weeks, even months?"

Robin knew instantly that she would. She had the strangest feeling that her entire life had been rather a dress rehearsal, preparing her for this moment. She was ready. She and Jackson were trying so hard to be gentle companions to their mother, at the end of her life. To hold Lydia in their hearts for as long as she was theirs. Couldn't they also do this for an AIDS victim, another child of God in desperate need? She knew if she rested her head on the Tabernacle, the answer would be yes.

"When you speak with—Philip and Johnathon, was it?—let them know that I have a spare bedroom and bath that is theirs, for as long as they'd like. Tell them it is an old family home, much in need of a family."

Father George nodded; he looked pleased, but not surprised.

"Tell me," he asked Robin. "Will you be disappointed if you don't see the saints any longer?"

She was startled by his question. "I don't know. I hadn't thought about it. Why do you ask?"

"Because," the priest explained, "I think you got their message."

Robin gazed across the cluttered room to where her favorite saint of all was placing the cork stopper back in the bottle. "It's all about love, little one," she pronounced, mimicking his voice.

He smiled at her, fondly.

CHAPTER THIRTEEN

ROBIN WALKED HOME FROM THE vicarage with a happier heart than she'd had in many months. She knew she was surrounded by love. How could she ever have forgotten it, she wondered.

As she walked through the peaceful neighborhood, she hummed a familiar old hymn, trying to recall the words. The best she could do was the one line that always made her cry: "...filled with His goodness, lost in His love." For, indeed, she was.

Alas, her happy mood was short-lived. As she entered the house, the phone began ringing. She rushed to answer it. The director at St. Vitus informed her that her mother had fallen again. Getting off the bus from the shopping trip, Lydia had missed a step. She had struck the back of her head on the pavement, bruising it severely. Thankfully, Miriam was behind her; the over-sized tote-bag she carried had broken Lydia's fall.

Even so, she had been taken to the hospital for observation. Lydia had eventually been released and was back at her apartment, resting. St. Vitus had been attempting to reach Robin all afternoon. She rushed to be with her mother.

Lydia was asleep, looking very old and fragile. Robin sat by her bed, holding her hand. The back of her head and neck were a deep purple.

When she awoke, she seemed completely defeated. "Oh, honey," she smiled in recognition, "I'm very sorry. I feel so stupid."

Robin assured her that there was no need to apologize. "You're not a bit stupid, Mom. You're simply old."

She stayed with her until late that night. Bringing her dinner; helping her to the bathroom; chatting about incidentals; finally tucking her into bed, with a mild sedative. As Lydia drifted off to sleep, she gazed at her oldest daughter, sadly. "I suppose I crushed my new hat when I fell. I'd just bought it. They packed it so carefully; in tissue paper…"

"No, Mom, it's fine—you fell backwards," Robin explained.

"Oh, good," she replied, sleepily. "At least I can still do something right."

Robin kissed her forehead, crying silently.

It was terribly late when she finally returned to her own home. Still, she picked up the telephone and dialed Jackson's number. She answered on the first ring.

"Of course we're still up! Sam is in his workshop, beavering away on some new inlay design. I'm providing refreshing beverages and witty banter!"

In spite of everything, Robin had to smile. Sam crafted gorgeous writing instruments—pens and pencils from exotic woods and stones. Fountain pens were his specialty. He was many years older than Jackson, and many years more serious.

They made a charming couple, complementing one another. She could just picture Sam, bending over some exacting tool…and Jackson, dancing in with a martini shaker. She hated to interrupt them.

"I'm afraid it's mom. She's fallen again." Robin told her about the accident.

"I'm coming down! Tomorrow!" Jack stated firmly.

Robin tried to convince her there was nothing she could do, but Jackson insisted.

"We can gang up on her!" Jack declared. "Present a solid front! Seriously, she needs to get used to a walker before something awful happens."

The truth was, Robin longed to see her sister, for her mother and for herself. So much had happened. So much was about to. And she wanted Jackson to be a part of it.

"I *would* love to see you, actually," she admitted, "but there is no hurry. When it's convenient, do come down. Your old room is always ready. We could have a long talk."

"I knew it!" Jackson squealed. "You're in love!"

Robin groaned.

"With Wheelchair Jim! Who could resist a man who throws up *on* his own balcony?!" her sister laughed merrily. "I'll see you by Friday and you can tell me all about him!"

"Jack," Robin sighed, "you are a fearful moron. And I love you so much. See you Friday."

CHAPTER FOURTEEN

As she replaced the receiver, Robin glanced at the mantel clock. She knew she should be tired but felt strangely on edge. She walked to the kitchen and put the kettle on.

Robin loaded a small tray with a restaurant-ware mug and teapot. She added a triangle of freshly baked shortbread, for good measure. Carrying the tray onto the wide front porch, she noticed it had begun to rain, making the night air pleasantly cool. She sat in the worn wicker rocker and sipped the herbal blend, hoping it would help her sleep.

The old house was silent except for the patter of the rain. Still, it felt to her a welcome place; the front door open, and the windows alight.

The house had been in the Landry family for generations. It seemed to have a life of its own, somehow. Or rather, it possessed a bit of all the lives that had shared its rooms.

Robin delighted in recalling her childhood days; poring over her earliest memories like well-worn flash cards. In the kitchen with her grandmother, Emily, baking Mardi Gras King Cakes…on the sidewalk with her cousins, learning to roller-skate…in the attic with the neighborhood children, exploring the contents of the many ancient trunks—what a happy, hectic place it always seemed.

Except, she remembered, when her mother had a migraine. Then the entire household tip-toed about, speaking in whispers, their noses buried in books. All of her friends knew that Lydia was tormented by monthly "episodes." They would still come to the house, so much did they feel drawn to its warmth, but they brought crayons or paints and quietly busied themselves, making gifts for the invalid. Robin and Jackson had discovered an entire box of artwork ("For Miss Lydia, With Love") from their childhood chums. Their favorite was a garishly gruesome depiction of Jesus, wearing a crown of thorns, done entirely in macaroni products.

Robin laughed out loud and nibbled a cookie. She could close her eyes and imagine the voices and laughter of her little friends.

The old house creaked and settled. She wondered if it felt lonely. Perhaps, she thought, it had been resting these past few years. Catching its breath. Bracing itself for the next generation of toddlers tripping down the front steps. The next cache of batons landing on its roof as little sisters practiced their tosses. Wondering where all the babies with skinned knees, in search of bandages and kisses, had gone.

"I'm afraid Jack and I have let you down, old place", Robin whispered, knowing how mawkish she sounded. As she stared into the falling rain, she saw another night, long ago, in the French Quarter.

Will had treated her to a weekend get-away, hoping to cheer her up. They had just learned, for certain, that they would never be parents. Hand in hand, they strolled the deserted streets, not feeling the rain as it soaked them. Not needing to speak. Everything had been said.

Without thinking, they turned into St. Louis Cathedral. Like the streets, it too was empty, save for one lone pilgrim. At the foot of the altar steps, not so much kneeling as curled into a fetal position, was a very young, very small adolescent. Robin and Will were deeply touched by the scene they had intruded upon. Its lesson did not escape them. Sorrowing as they were, because they had no child…and here was a child, seemingly quite alone in the world.

"We stumble upon them every day," Will would later say, "if only we have eyes to see."

They returned to Baton Rouge with happy hearts; their eyes ever open, vowing to watch for the least of these. Through the years, their joy increased as they cultivated the habit of viewing any child in need as their very own.

Thunder softly sounded in the distance, drawing Robin back to the familiar front porch. She rose and stretched. Gathering the mug and teapot, she headed to bed at last, careful to leave the front door open and the porch light on. "Just in case," she whispered to the night.

CHAPTER FIFTEEN

JACKSON ARRIVED AS PROMISED THE following Friday, bearing gifts. Champagne, cheeses, chocolates, and a radiant smile. She would have brought more, but her car was filled with her extensive wardrobe and photography equipment. In all her travels, she had never learned to pack light. On car trips, she simply kept throwing things in until the spaces were full.

She was thrilled to hear of the imminent arrival of Philip and Johnathon. Even more so, after speaking to them on the telephone. "Did you know that they owned their own catering business in Atlanta? Pip says he'll teach me to make omelets that float off the plate!" she enthused.

"Pip?!" Robin teased.

"Philip. Pip. You know. He said that when John became ill, people began avoiding them and business evaporated. Can you believe how ignorant people are?! Like you can catch AIDS from heirloom tomato bruschetta! I mean, really!"

Robin had heard the story from Philip, too. He and John had sold their catering company, Petit Fleur, when it became obvious that John would not recover. Even people who knew it was irrational felt frightened when they saw how thin John was, and how sad Philip often seemed. "No one wants their joyous occasion planned and executed by two ghouls, darling!" Pip laughed; but he was serious. "Are you sure you won't mind us invading your house? I can assure you, we're absolutely horrifying!"

After several such telephone calls, Robin and Jackson convinced them that they would be welcome. "You'll fit right in," Robin overheard Jack, speaking in confidential tones. "Robin has always been prone to depression. If not for my unflagging good spirits and sparkling personality, she would have ended her life in a convent. I'd hate to see that happen to you and John!" Robin smiled to herself. She was so glad Jack was home.

The previous day, they had moved Robin's things out of the downstairs bedroom. Johnathon required a place on the ground floor. They gave the room a thorough cleaning and airing, then filled it with fresh linen and flowers. The two girls were upstairs, in the rooms they had grown up in, sharing a "Jack and Jill" bath.

They both talked, late into the night, about their mother and about the boys. Robin related the fantastic tale of Gabriel and the saints, recounting all that Father George had said. Jackson had listened to this in wide-eyed wonder. She considered it all for quite some time. At last she said, "I'm amazed at what you've told me, of course. And baffled, frankly. But I don't doubt it; not for one moment! I can see that it has made you very happy, and I won't say a word against it. You go on living among the saints. And ask them to pray for me!"

CHAPTER SIXTEEN

Seven. Seven separate creams and lotions. Robin was chagrinned as she counted them all. *That's what it takes for me to look presentable these days*, she thought. One less, and I look like Ernest Borgnine. She hurried to apply the last one, so the shared bathroom would be free for her sister.

Robin placed her ear to the bedroom door, to see if Jack was stirring; she was surprised to hear her speaking into the telephone, heatedly. Robin quickly turned and withdrew to her own room.

It wasn't long until a faint tapping brought her to the door. It was obvious that Jackson had been crying. As the two girls flopped onto the bed, Jack pummeled the pillows violently.

"Sam wants me to come home! Immediately! He doesn't think that I should be involved in any of this! He says Pip and Johnathon could be dangerous!" she wailed.

Robin couldn't help laughing. "Oh, for crying out loud! Dangerous?!"

"It's always been so easy for you!" Jackson cried. "Will was such a sweet, gentle man. All he ever wanted in life was for you to be happy."

Robin was stunned. "I'm sure Sam wants your happiness—"

"Sam wants me," Jackson replied, "not my happiness. There's a big difference."

Robin was confused. She poured her sobbing sister a glass of water from the bedside carafe. Jack gulped and hiccoughed.

"I know it sounds insane, but Sam thinks if I care for anyone else, I somehow care less for him. Any friendships I cultivate make him uneasy."

"I had no idea," Robin murmured.

"I try to tell myself it's not a big deal," Jackson sniffed. She sighed deeply. "It's Luke I miss the most…"

Little Luke. The pasta artist. It was he who had produced the portrait of our suffering Lord for Lydia. Robin had not thought of him for years.

"The last time I saw Luke was at your wedding reception," she said.

"Me, too," Jackson responded, sadly. "Sam can't stand him. Every time I try to see Luke, or even talk about him, Sam goes ballistic."

Luke and Jackson had been best friends since before elementary school. They had shared so many good times. So much laughter. Robin smiled as she pictured the two of them, through the years—as playmates, as schoolmates… as soul mates. Each of their lives would have been so much less without the other.

"But why?" she asked. "Why doesn't Sam like Luke?"

"Because *I* do," Jackson replied, flatly. "And it's not just Luke. I've lost track of all the friends I've neglected, to make Sam happy. He wants me all to himself. All of me. All the time," she concluded.

"So it's not Pip and John that he finds dangerous...it's your love for them?!" Robin was appalled at the concept.

Jackson shared her horror. "I know. It's all so wrong. I'm just figuring it out, myself." She sighed again.

"Whenever I would mention the possibility of adopting a child, Sam would sulk for days. Pouting and moping about. Then he'd come up with excuses—his age, his retirement plans, our finances; but I think the thought of sharing me, even with a baby, terrified him. That was the worst."

"I never realized," whispered Robin.

"Why would you? Until now, I've always given in. It just didn't seem worth fighting over. But this time, I'm staying! I'm a part of this!"

Tears began to stream down her face. "And I just screamed at Sam that he's a part of it, too."

Robin held her, rocking her softly. "I'm sure he'll come around." She tried her best to sound convincing. "He loves you so much...he just doesn't have a goddamn clue what that means!"

Jackson threw a pillow at her sister, pulled the quilt over her head, and spent the rest of the morning in bed.

At last, the smell of cinnamon and vanilla lured her downstairs where Robin was waiting in the kitchen. The sisters smiled at one another, across the old wood table. For a brief moment, they could almost see their dear papa at one end and Lydia at the other; Will beside Robin, grinning contentedly; and little Luke, chatting to Jack. They both laughed, simultaneously.

Robin plunged a serving spoon into a pale blue Fire King baking dish. "I've always thought," she said, hopefully, "that warm bread pudding provides a comfort denied even to prayer."

Jackson accepted the bowl, gratefully. "It's the whiskey sauce," she replied, with a forlorn grin.

Robin handed her the bowl and ladle. "Have as much as you'd like."

CHAPTER SEVENTEEN

So it was that Robin and Jackson were both at home when the boys finally arrived. Even if Jack had returned to Houston, she would have made another trek, so attached had she become to the entire idea. "It's just like the Under-Ground Railroad," Robin heard her laughing into the telephone, "and dear Pip is Harriet Tubman!"

The sisters were waiting on the front porch when the rental car from Baton Rouge pulled into the driveway. As much as they had tried to prepare themselves, the sight of Johnathon was still a shock. He was tall and painfully thin. His skin had a grey pallor and was mottled with bruises. His eyes were huge and gentle but looked very tired. His appearance seemed especially heart-breaking as it was easy to imagine how handsome he must've been, at one time. He had a large, classic nose and a lovely, wide grin. Robin took his hands in hers, kissed him on the cheek, and whispered, "We're so happy you're here." Jackson hugged him soundly.

Philip slid out from behind the wheel, beaming. "At last!" he enthused. He and Jackson began unloading the SUV, chatting like old friends. "I wasn't sure what we'd need, so I brought a little of everything! Don't you just love these old houses?! I feel like I'm in Mayberry! My dear, you're exactly like I pictured you—a little Catholic schoolgirl!"

Robin led Johnathon carefully up the walk, taking his arm. "You must forgive Philip. When he gets nervous, he babbles. There's no silencing him, I'm afraid."

"He's perfectly fine," Robin assured him. "It's nice having a child about the place."

John laughed, "He's 32! But you're right—there's a lot of Peter Pan in him."

"And a little Wendy!" Philip called over. John rolled his eyes, good-naturedly.

"Would you like tea?" Jackson offered. "It's all set." She walked by, with two small suitcases. "Or would you like to rest a while? Traveling can be exhausting, I know." Johnathon and Philip agreed that tea sounded perfect.

Philip was the smaller of the two, as well as the younger. His hair was blond and wavy; his eyes a deep blue. When he laughed, which he did often, his entire face looked angelic.

He and Jackson were busy rummaging about, laying out the tea service. Robin was comfortable, attending to Johnathon; settling him into an over-stuffed chair near the coffee table. "Clotted cream!" Pip squealed from the kitchen.

"And Robin's home-made lemon curd," Jackson added. "Yum!"

"Now I know I'm going to love it here!" Philip hugged Jackson and feigned a grab for the raspberry jam.

"Would you prefer herbal tea or black?" Jackson inquired of Johnathon.

"Oh, black is perfect. At this stage, it's too late to worry about herbal benefits, I'm afraid."

"STOP!" Pip screeched, dramatically. "We agreed not to be morbid for the entire time we're here! Otherwise, I'll start crying and I'll never stop! And this is to be a happy occasion, sooo—" he grinned outlandishly and reached for the teapot, "I'll pour, shall I?"

Johnathon accepted a cup. "These are beautiful. Were they your mother's?"

"Actually, no." Robin inspected the cup and saucer she held. "Will and I collected them. We loved old things and surrounded ourselves with flea-market finds. British, a plus."

Jackson added, "Robin and Will were Luddites. They think modern inventions are of the devil!"

"Surely not the Slap-Chop?!" Philip interjected. Robin and Jackson disintegrated into laughter. John shook his head, in disbelief. "I warn you, don't encourage him."

After the four new friends had finished the tea and scones, it was obvious that John was in need of a rest. Robin showed him to his room, explaining where the towels were kept and leaving bottled water on the nightstand. "More than anything," she said, as she turned to leave, "we want you to feel at home."

"Robin," he called, "stay with me a moment." He fell onto the turned-down bed, gazing at the ceiling. "Thank you for not being terribly horrified."

"Horrified? At what?"

He smiled a sad smile. "At me, of course." He touched his cheeks. "A face only a mother could love. And in my case, not even that. She and my father told me to leave, you know."

Robin took his hands and gently lowered them. Her own fingers stroked his handsome nose. "I can't speak as a mother," she told him, firmly, "but how about a friend? I think I could find your face very easy to love. Give me, oh, about five more minutes."

He sighed, happily, and dozed.

Jackson and Pip had cleared away the tea things. It was clear that Jack had made another conquest; they were already great chums. He was examining all the retro bric-a-brac throughout the house.

"This is fabulous! It's like being in a time warp. And you actually use it all! I can't believe I'll be eating breakfast off Melmac—the space-age, unbreakable Polymer!"

"I know that's always been a dream of mine!" Jackson teased.

"Oh, my gawd! A rotary telephone!" He hurried to the ringing device. "Let me answer it! I beg of you!"

Of course they did, to Pip's delight. It was Father George. They arranged to meet late that afternoon.

Robin excused herself, intending to run up to St. Vitus' Village; but Philip insisted on meeting their mother. They left a note for John, in case he awoke. "He won't, for several hours; it's getting so he sleeps more and more. I sit and watch him. I'm so afraid I'll forget what he looks like. I try to memorize every detail. How his eyelashes lay on his cheeks; how his lips turn up, just slightly—he was so beautiful, you know…" Pip talked as they strolled.

"But more than that, he's wise and he's kind. When we met, I was just a silly kid; going from lover to lover, like you do. Thinking I'd always be 18 and fabulous. John warned me that it could be a hard life. I needed to learn to support myself. So I went to culinary school and we started our catering business. Would you believe it—we have been together almost every minute, for the last seven years; and I've never grown tired of him. Even more amazing, he's never grown tired of me! That's when it struck me—Philip, you freak, this is love! This is what everyone is searching for! And it fell into my lap. I think I must be the luckiest person in the world." He broke down and sobbed.

Through her own tears, Jackson did her best to mimic her little friend's decree, "STOP! We agreed not to be morbid!" her voice cracked. "This is to be a happy occasion."

Philip wiped his eyes on his abundant sleeve-length, took the girls' hands, and they walked through the gates of St. Vitus Village.

CHAPTER EIGHTEEN

Lydia was still unsteady on her feet after the fall from the bus steps. The bruising was paler, but had spread from her head and neck to her shoulders. She was sitting up in bed, reading tabloids, when the girls arrived with Philip.

That habit had begun with Robin and Jackson, much to their chagrin. They became hooked on the outlandish magazines after seeing an article referring to Luciano Pavarotti (whom they worshipped) as a Two Ton Tenor. "Two Ton Tenor Builds Whale of a Gym!" the headline screamed at them. Since that atrocity, they wouldn't think of visiting one another without an arm-load of the papers. Unfortunately, Lydia began coveting them for their serious news reporting.

She was pleased to see her two daughters; and when she learned who Philip was, she was overjoyed. No celebrity from her gossip rags could have thrilled her more.

"We all knew you'd be here soon! I bought a new dress for the service; it's a lovely silver-grey color," she informed

Philip, who had pulled a chair close to her bed. "And what will you and Johnathon be wearing?"

He was happy to go over their wardrobe, in detail. Robin and Jackson exchanged bemused glances as the two discussed hairstyles, footwear, and make-up. Lydia insisted on getting up to locate her hat, for Pip's approval, but found herself barely able to balance. As Pip helped her back into bed ("Think nothing of it, my dear—I have lots of experience at this"), she wailed, "Oh, Philip! What if I'm not able to go to your wedding? I'll be so disappointed!"

"WAIT!" Pip shouted. "I have it! You need a walker. Of course—you can have Johnathon's! You *shall* go to the ball, Cinderella!" he pronounced, hugging her.

Lydia looked helplessly at Robin and Jackson, who were struggling to keep from laughing.

"I couldn't, really," she managed to squeak.

"Nonsense," replied Philip. "It's a wonderful thing. State of the art. Very lightweight, with a small seat, and—"

"But…I mean …won't John need it?" Lydia made one last attempt.

"I only wish he did." Philip looked so sad. "I'm afraid he's past that now. He seemed to go from walking quite briskly to needing a wheelchair for any distance. I had so hoped that the walker would help him keep up with me, for even a few more months. I'd love to think you were getting some use out of it." He sniffed. "It's maroon and would be lovely with silver-grey…"

What could she say? The girls were stunned to hear her thank him sincerely and promise to treasure it. They avoided meeting one another's eyes; they knew they were inches away from giggling, uncontrollably. Robin buried her nose in a tabloid and Jackson gazed out the bedroom window. Pip and Lydia made arrangements to have the walker delivered to the Village the next day.

Before returning home, the three went by the chapel. Philip judged it "perfectly charming." He reverently bowed to the altar, to the girls' approval. They had ascertained that he was Episcopalian; but more than that, they did not know. Father George, however, got directly to the heart of the matter when he visited that afternoon.

CHAPTER NINETEEN

JOHN APPEARED A BIT MORE rested when the priest arrived. He had napped, and showered, and was dressed rather formally. Philip, too, had showered; but was casual, in blue jeans. They sat, side by side, holding hands.

Father George seemed truly happy to meet them at last. His tone set a mood of gracious acceptance, as Robin and Jack knew it would. The sisters offered to leave them alone; but that suggestion was immediately vetoed, to their delight.

Father George and Robin sipped their usual Scotch; Jackson and Pip, gin; Johnathon had a dry white wine. "I'm on so many meds," he explained, "it limits my choice of alcohol. Though I do wonder, actually, what's the worst that could happen?"

"I'm so sorry." It was clear Father George had thought of saying more…but what?

Pip and John both thanked him, simultaneously; then smiled at one another.

"Please tell me about your…faith journey—heavens, I hate that term! Were you raised in the church?"

Philip, as he related, was a cradle Episcopalian. He loved everything about it—the liturgy, the music, the beautiful ceremonies; but mostly, the weekly Eucharist, or Holy Communion. He truly felt he knew Jesus in the breaking of bread.

"I, on the other hand," explained Johnathon, "came to the Episcopal faith later; after meeting Philip, actually." John was the adopted child of a Mormon couple, raised, of course, in that denomination. "When I finally told them that I was gay, they cut all ties. It was horrible. Especially Mom. I couldn't believe that she could simply stop loving me. For any reason."

Philip interrupted, "Let alone just because you dressed well, had a tastefully decorated home, and could dance divinely!"

John blushed, but looked fondly at his intended. "Pip's love for the Episcopal church (and more than that—his love for Christ and Our Lady) so impressed me. Let's face it—you *have* to know this one is gay as soon as he opens his mouth," (Pip feigned surprise), "yet he is at home in a church pew. That floored me. I needed that. Perhaps more so, when I discovered how ill I was. I was confirmed five years ago; and we've been attending Mass every week since."

"However," Philip said, pointedly, "it hasn't all been smooth sailing! John ended up keeping me from storming out of the sanctuary more times than I can recall!"

"Pip, please. It doesn't matter," John sighed.

"It matters!" Pip was trying to control himself. He lowered his voice and took a deep breath. "I had told

Johnathon how special my church was. You can be different in any number of ways; but we are all the same when we kneel to receive the Body of Christ, at the altar. We are all welcome. Until New Hampshire dared to choose a gay man as their bishop!"

Father George was listening intently, glass held between his hands. "Ahhh, I see," he murmured.

"Do you?" asked Philip. "Our church immediately started having meetings to decide what they thought of all this; what they should do. People who I thought loved John and me said the ugliest things. Stupid things!"

Johnathon interrupted, "That's enough, Sweetheart." He tried to soften Pip's words. "Perhaps it was easier for me. I'd been through it before, with my parents. You know—'Come back when you're straight; then you can be a part of our family again.' But I knew God didn't love like that. I was convinced that we'd find a way if we just kept trying."

"Crystal Blue Persuasion," Robin muttered. The boys looked puzzled.

Father George explained, "Love is the answer to every equation."

"You sound like Pip," Johnathon smiled. "He was on his feet at every parish meeting, insisting that God's love is everything."

"And the *only* thing," Pip added.

John kissed his lover's hand. "Did I ever tell you how proud I was of you?" he asked.

Pip pouted. "For all the good it did. Half of the church eventually left, re-forming under some hateful African bishop. Even then, I tried to keep in touch, visiting their new church. I cared for them and missed them, in spite of everything. And I needed to go for myself; to see if all I had argued for was possible. And to forgive." He sighed. "But then came the most ghastly development of all, at the new church!"

"Oh, no," Robin braced herself.

"Yes!" Pip continued, with a gleam in his eye. "Praise choruses with the words projected on a giant screen! The Kyrie set to a reggae beat!" He gave a blood-curdling scream, as the assembled group howled with laughter.

After some measure of decorum was restored, plans were made for the blessing of their union. Robin and Jackson assured Johnathon that there was no hurry, hoping his strength might return after a few days of settling in. Philip and Father George agreed. In the end, they decided on an evening service, in three days. A very small affair. "But loads of flowers!" declared Pip. "I want the residents to keep them; it will brighten up their apartments."

The evening ended cheerfully. Johnathon was propped on the sofa, covered with a throw; while the others played a spirited game of Scrabble. Father George won easily. But only, Pip insisted, "By cheating! Latin shouldn't count!"

CHAPTER TWENTY

Far from regaining his strength, Johnathon grew weaker with each passing day. Though no one spoke of it, they all realized. They did their best to see that he had everything he needed; mostly, their company. Even as he appeared to doze, John would smile weakly, hearing Pip and Jackson arguing over the last piece of Sticky Toffee Pudding—"We'll cast lots for it!"—and Robin finally telling them to divide the damned thing.

To everyone's amazement, Johnathon managed to rally on the night of the service. Though he arrived in a wheelchair, he looked rested and utterly content. Philip was thrilled at his transformation. Both men donned exquisite dark suits, crisp white shirts, and lovely patterned neck ties. A small white rose bud was on each lapel. It was altogether elegant.

Philip insisted on getting Johnathon to the chapel by himself. "We have some things we need to say; we'd like to be alone for a few moments. Please tell me you understand." Of course, they did.

The sisters left early to collect Lydia. She had spent the previous day getting used to her new walker. She proudly emerged from her bedroom, looking very pretty indeed. "See how easily it glides!" she exclaimed.

Jackson never looked lovelier, in a pale pink suit; her blonde hair brushed to a luxurious shine. Robin had chosen a bronze sheath; very retro and flattering to her willowy figure. The only touch of color was a vintage beaded clutch (containing a handful of tissues).

Robin was thinking how much she longed for Will. He would have loved the boys. Jackson somehow realized this and stayed very close to her dear sister, frequently taking her arm. She knew that later that night, she would quietly pad across the shared bathroom, to join Robin in the big iron bed (as her older sister had often done for her, growing up).

The chapel was exquisite, filled with white flowers and white hair. Vases of blossoms were in every alcove and niche—roses, lilies, tulips, carnations, snap-dragons, spider-mums—the glow from the candles gave everything a warm, golden hue.

Almost every pew was taken by the residents of St. Vitus; which is quite an accomplishment, in a memory-care unit. Robin and Jackson had speculated on how many guests had waited patiently the previous evening; and how many would arrive the following night.

Miriam had saved Lydia a seat on the aisle, so her new walker wouldn't cause a commotion in the narrow pew. Robin and Jack took their seats in the first row.

Just before the hour, Father George made his way to the front of the church. He was dressed simply, in a long, black cassock; it was a perfect choice for the tall cleric. He knelt at the *prie dieu* to the side of the platform, in silent prayer. Jackson nudged her sister. "Nice touch!" Robin swatted at her, giggling.

Right on time, Philip entered from the back of the church, with John leaning heavily on him. Father George met them in front of the altar. The congregation was silent. The priest began, his voice steady and confident.

"A reading from Saint Paul's epistle to the Corinthians, beginning at the 31st verse of the 12th chapter: 'And I will show you a still more excellent way—'"

Robin heard a loud rustling from the back of the sanctuary; then the shuffling of feet. She turned. Standing behind the pews were her new friends, Gabriel, Francis, Veronica, Fiacre, and others she didn't recognize, all smiling sweetly. Jackson gave her a quizzical look and touched her arm, softly. Apparently, she had heard and seen nothing. Only Father George paused for a moment and seemed to be hiding a grin.

He began again, "And I will show you a still more excellent way. If I speak in the tongues of mortals and angels, but do not have love, I am a noisy gong or a clanging cymbal. And if I have prophetic powers and understand all mysteries and all knowledge, and if I have all faith, so as to remove mountains, but do not have love, I am nothing. If I give away all my possessions, and if I hand over my body so that I may boast, but do not have love, I gain nothing. Love is patient; love is kind; love is not envious or boastful or arrogant or rude. It does not insist on its own way; it is not irritable or resentful; it does not rejoice in wrongdoing, but rejoices in the truth. It bears all things, believes all things, hopes all things, endures all things. Love never ends."

Pip and John had been gazing at one another, as Father George read. Now they knelt before him. He placed their hands together, binding them with a beautifully embroidered strip of cloth. He touched their hands with his own and pronounced God's blessing upon them. Except for a spontaneous kiss, that was the entire service.

Then the celebration began! Most of the residents had not met John; they lined up to give him their sincere best wishes. He seemed to treasure each word. Pip, meanwhile, was happily distributing the floral arrangements and thanking everyone for attending. They couldn't get enough of him.

At last, the crowd dispersed and the friends, accompanied by Father George, escorted the happy couple home. Champagne had been chilled and was poured into flutes. Philip and Johnathon had made a point that no gifts were to be given ("You've done so much for us already"), but there was one lavishly wrapped present awaiting them. It was, of course, a Slap-Chop.

John was obviously on the verge of exhaustion. After one toast, he excused himself and started for their bedroom. "Please, Philip, stay up, if you'd like. Enjoy the champagne."

"Are you mad?!" Pip screamed. "On my wedding night?!"

John laughed, "Come along, then; but I fear you'll be disappointed."

Pip grabbed the bottle and two glasses, trilling, "I'll be the judge of that!"

As the little group watched them go, Johnathon bracing himself against his lover, his expression one of infinite tenderness, the priest declared, "If any one of you put a stumbling block before one of these little ones who believe in me, it would be better for you if a great mill-stone were fastened around your neck, and you were drowned in the depths of the sea."

Robin had never before heard Father George utter such a harsh word. Jackson, too, looked startled. She asked, seriously, "Is that in keeping with love, dear Father?"

"It was Love, Himself, who first said it," was his only reply.

CHAPTER TWENTY-ONE

THE FOLLOWING MORNING, ROBIN AND Jackson awoke to the smell of bacon frying, bread toasting, and coffee brewing. They tumbled down the stairs, in pajamas and slippers, to discover Pip in the kitchen. "I'm thinking full English breakfast!" he announced. The girls quickly sat down at the table.

As Pip handed each a plate, he told them, solemnly, "Last night was absolutely perfect. Exactly what John and I wanted. How can we ever thank you?"

The girls looked at one another. "How about," said Jackson, pondering, "by passing the butter. I think that ought to make us about even!"

"Au contraire! You let him off too easily," laughed Robin. "Ask for the marmalade, too!"

The subject was closed.

Breakfast was delicious and they lingered over it. Philip took tea and toast to John, who hardly touched it.

Pip didn't need to ask—his friends would have been insulted if he had—it was just assumed that he and John would be staying. They had found their home; and their family.

Jackson, however, began packing after breakfast. She had been away from Sam much longer than she had anticipated. They had not spoken since their last angry telephone conversation. She missed him dreadfully, but hated to say goodbye to Pip, and especially to John. She made Robin swear to call her the minute they feared death was imminent.

"First, me; *then* Father George," she stressed. "I have farther to come!"

As she lugged her suitcases down the stairs, there was a knock at the door. Standing on the porch was Jackson's husband, Sam. "Surprise!" he exclaimed. "Is there room for one more?"

The look on his wife's face answered his question. She ran into his arms, chattering, "Of course! You don't take up much space! But what—?"

Sam explained, "I knew you wanted to stay until—well, a while longer; and I thought, *why not?* I can re-arrange my schedule. Besides, I haven't met the newlyweds!"

Robin hugged her brother-in-law, so thankful that he had come. They unpacked his car. He'd done his best to bring things he thought Jack might need, as well as his own necessities.

At the earliest opportunity, Robin slipped away, joining Pip and Johnathon in their bedroom. She quietly explained that Sam had arrived and would, she felt, appreciate a few moments alone with his wife. The very idea sent Pip into gales of laughter and frenzied activity, as he peeped through key-holes and listened through walls. Robin and John studiously ignored his antics.

Alone at last, Sam gathered Jackson into his arms. She started to speak, but he tenderly laid his fingertips over her lips.

"Please. Let me." Sam drew several deep breaths. Jackson had never seen so many emotions play across his face; she found it impossible to determine the dominant one. Eventually, he seemed to master them; quietly, he asked his wife, "Can you ever forgive me for being so foolish? For thinking that in loving others, you somehow loved me less?"

Jackson had prepared herself for many things—explanations, accusations, even indifference; but this painfully accurate confession took her completely by surprise. She found herself speechless.

Sam continued, "After we spoke on the phone, I was furious. And frightened. I began to drink. By afternoon, I was plastered, I'm ashamed to say." He grimaced at the memory.

"Perhaps it was the alcohol… or simply a dream—or both; I don't know. But I somehow felt I was visited by Saint Joseph." He turned away, blushing.

"I believe you," Jackson whispered. Her words were filled with such tenderness, it touched her husband deeply. He was determined to continue with his narrative.

"Joseph sat with me for quite a while, assuring me that he knew how I felt. How just when we think our lives are mapped out, following our carefully laid plans, Love steps in, compelling us to go in another direction. He said we'd both been given wives who instinctively understood this. He picked up the picture of you; the one I keep on my nightstand. He smiled so sweetly and said, 'If I had not learned to trust…oh, the love I would never have known! Oh, the wonders I would never have seen!'"

Sam grinned, sheepishly. "To tell the truth, I didn't quite understand what he was getting at. Perhaps I didn't want to. He tried one more time to make me see. His voice was so gentle, but so firm. I will never forget his warning—'The heart of a woman is a wonderful thing. Especially one so completely open to Love. If you force her to close it, you will break it.'" Sam choked back his tears.

"Oh, Jacksie, his words have haunted me for days. I've tried to hoard your love, afraid that it might slip away. I wanted to close your heart; and close our home." He struggled to finish his thoughts.

"As Saint Joseph left, he turned and asked, 'Until you learn to trust Jackson, can you trust me?' I'm determined to try, my darling. Will you help me?"

"We'll help each other," Jackson assured him, "And God will help us both."

Sam embraced his wife. He kissed her hair again and again, breathing in its sweet familiar fragrance. Finally he whispered, "Just promise me one thing—if Love sends us into Egypt, fleeing for our lives, promise me you'll let me do the packing!"

At that moment, Philip burst into the room; he smirked at the embracing couple and suggested loudly, "Get a room!"

After introductions were made and pleasantries exchanged, the happy pair slipped upstairs, eager to take his advice.

CHAPTER TWENTY-TWO

SAM WAS AN EXCELLENT COOK, especially the Cajun dishes he had grown up with. He and Pip immediately hit it off and began planning meals and compiling grocery lists.

Sam's real talent, though, was telling stories. He was entertaining and amusing, with a repertoire of tales from his days traveling the globe, when he and Jack were young.

Sam sat for hours with Johnathon, describing idyllic scenes on Grand Cayman and Bonaire, not minding when he fell asleep. He'd gently straighten the quilts, dim the lights, and tip-toe out to locate his wife.

Philip, of course, begged him to tell of his dating days, laughing maniacally if he slipped and revealed some secret from Jackson's past.

They all took turns keeping John company, as much for their sake as for his. Even during the final weeks, he was unfailingly sweet and pleasant.

His favorite visitor, though, turned out to be their mother, Lydia. She would sit next to his bed, whispering to him, giggling like a teenager, and taking notes. None of them knew exactly what they discussed; they heard only snippets. Mostly, plans for the afterlife—what an adventure it would be: who they hoped to meet, who they'd try to avoid. Pip teased them both, certain that they were up to no good. "Admit it! You're planning a murder/suicide pact! At least have the decency to tell me if I'm the victim!" Lydia would roll her eyes and smile.

On occasion, usually just at twilight, Johnathon would slip into a singular state of mind and call quietly for his mother. Philip's attempts at determining which mother—birth or adoptive—only seemed to agitate John. Thankfully, Lydia would step in, somehow discerning which role to play.

As the others watched, spell-bound, she seemed to slip effortlessly from John's young mother, who kept him less than a year, to the mother who raised him, to the Blessed Virgin, Mother of us all, and back to herself, seated at his bedside.

With only slight adaptations, her words were always the same, gently repeated: "Johnathon, I loved you from the moment you were placed in my arms"—here Lydia would substitute *in the hospital, at your christening, when we adopted you,* or *the day you arrived in Fairhope...*—"Not for one moment have I ever stopped. You must forgive me if it ever appeared otherwise."

Without fail, these words reassured Johnathon and he would slip into a restful night. Somehow, the others were equally comforted. Lydia, losing so many facets of her life to the dark void of Alzheimers, was quietly overjoyed to discover, intact, her familiar and favorite role as Mum.

When asked how she knew which mother John needed, Lydia thought for a long moment. Her face appeared happy and sad at the same time. "They're all the same, really," was the closest she could come to an explanation.

Johnathon's nightstand was crowded with prescription drug bottles. Philip had worked out elaborate systems, to be certain all the tablets and liquids were taken as directed. At last, it became obvious to them that they weren't helping. John would turn away from the proffered drug and request a kiss on the forehead instead. He grew weaker each day.

CHAPTER TWENTY-THREE

Early one morning, Pip emerged from the bedroom and walked slowly into the kitchen, where the others were having breakfast. He moved as though in a trance; all color had drained from his face. Jackson rushed to his side, as Robin pulled out a chair. Sam, too, was on his feet. "Please," Pip stammered, "call Father George. John says…oh, please, call him now."

Father George had been a regular visitor. He brought the Sacrament to John and Philip at least once a week. But they all knew that this was different. John had requested Extreme Unction—the last rites. Philip crumpled into Jackson's arms. Sam was on the phone to the priest. Robin walked calmly into the bedroom, to wait with John. She felt her heart was shattering.

His face was gaunt—his body skeletal. She could barely see his chest rise and fall; but she could hear his labored breathing. As she sat beside him, his eyes opened and he tried to smile. Robin began to weep.

She forced herself to pray. "Soul of Christ, sanctify me. Body of Christ, save me. Blood of Christ, inebriate me. Water from the side of Christ, cleanse me. Passion of Christ, strengthen me. Oh good Jesus, hear me. Within Thy wounds, hide me. Suffer me never to be separated from Thee. From the malicious foe defend me. And at the hour of my death, call me and bid me come to Thee, that with Thy saints, I may praise Thee, forever and ever. Amen." John squeezed her hand. She heard Father George and Pip slip into the room. She left them to their sad assignment.

Johnathon lingered through the afternoon. One by one, they bid him farewell, willing themselves to let him go. Sam brought Lydia to the house, returning her to St. Vitus' later that evening, along with Father George. Surprisingly, she seemed to accept that it was time for them to part. "Just a little while," she whispered, kissing his dear face. "I'll see you soon."

In the end, only Pip was with him when he breathed his last breath. He didn't have to tell them. When he walked out of the room, his face was already a mask of loneliness. He sat on the sofa, between Jackson and Robin. Several times, he started to speak, but could not. Finally, he told them, "Just before he died, he opened his eyes. Those beautiful dark eyes. And he said, "Oh, Pip…it's Love." And I said, "It's lovely? What's lovely?" But he shook his head; he said, "No. Not lovely. It's Love."

Pip stood and said that he wanted a shower, and then he'd like to sleep—could one of them take care of things for a while? He started up the stairs, walking slowly, as though each step required his last ounce of strength.

CHAPTER TWENTY-FOUR

In the days before the funeral, Philip spent his time almost entirely in the kitchen. He prepared lavish and elegant dishes, which he never touched. Although the rest of the family had little appetite, they ate with gusto, sensing that it pleased him. Sam was his only companion as he cooked, instinctively realizing that the intricate recipes and techniques kept Pip's mind occupied.

"He needs to be busy," Sam explained to the concerned sisters. "When he feels like talking, I listen; when he feels like crying, I hold him; mostly, I wash an awful lot of dishes!" he chuckled. Jackson beamed at her husband and told him, not for the first time, what a good father he would have made. Sam sighed, "If it hurts this much to lose one…"

At that moment, they all realized what John had become to them.

If Pip ate little, he seemed to sleep even less. Night after night, Jackson heard him talking to Robin in the next room…or pacing, in his own.

The funeral service was to be a private one. In the chapel, of course, followed by the committal at the gravesite. To everyone's surprise except Lydia's, John had asked to be buried in their family cemetery, just outside of Fairhope.

"He told me he wanted to be surrounded by us, just like these last few months. I promised him that I would be next," Lydia stated matter-of-factly, "so don't get any ideas! We have it all planned."

Philip hugged her, laughing. "I knew you two were up to something."

CHAPTER TWENTY-FIVE

THE MORNING OF THE FUNERAL, Jackson rose hours before dawn. She had her heart set on spending time alone in the chapel, where John's body had been placed. As she entered, she couldn't help but think how different the sanctuary looked. It was stripped of all flowers; the altar was bare; no candles glowed. John's plain casket was covered with a dark cloth. The only illumination was the red altar lamp and the moonlight through the windows.

Jackson slipped into a pew, bowed her head, and began to cry. For John, of course, and for Pip; for Robin, without Will; for Lydia, at the end of her life; for the baby that she and Sam would never hold; for gay children, on their own in this world; and finally for herself, sitting in a dark church, waiting to be comforted.

Eventually, she sensed that she was no longer alone. She lifted her head and peered around the moonlit chapel. By John's casket knelt a young woman. Her face—her entire being—was one of profound serenity. She was breathtakingly beautiful. And lost in prayer.

How long Jackson gazed at her, she couldn't say. She felt as if she had met her before; but could not recall the occasion. She had an overpowering desire to renew their acquaintance, but was loath to interrupt her prayers.

The woman turned toward Jackson and smiled. "She appeared so amiable," Jack would later tell her sister, "that I dared to ask if she knew John."

She laughed, as if the question was absurd. "But it didn't seem odd to hear her laughing; not out of place, I mean. It was the sweetest sound. Like—"

Robin interrupted, "Like clear water flowing over rocks?!"

That is exactly what Jackson had pictured in her mind—a merrily flowing stream.

Although Jackson knew the funeral was to be a small, private affair, she asked the visitor if she would be there. Quietly, she replied, "Of course."

Hearing her voice erased all doubts. Jackson's ocean-green eyes grew round with wonder and joy. She rose and, with a most reverent bow, whispered, "I will leave you to your prayers, Blessed Mother."

Ever after, the two sisters would laugh together that although Robin had made the acquaintance of saints and angels, Jackson had been dealt the trump card.

CHAPTER TWENTY-SIX

FATHER GEORGE OFFICIATED AT THE small service that morning. Philip sat beside Robin, holding tightly to her hand. They were both aware that she, too, had lost her spouse not so very long ago; their shared sorrow bound them together. Next to them were Sam and Jackson, their own hearts breaking with their loss. Beside her daughters, on the aisle, sat Lydia, fondly stroking her beloved walker. In the pew directly behind them, invisible to all, sat a young woman in a dark blue cloak, shimmering in the sunlight through the windows, and her angelic companion.

As the service progressed, the words began to have their intended effect. The priest could sense the change in his friends, as their faces relaxed and their responses grew steady. "All we go down to the dust; yet even at the grave, we make our song: Alleluia, Alleluia, Alleluia." He knew they meant the words they recited.

After seeing Lydia back to her apartment, the little band of mourners walked to the cemetery, allowing time for John's coffin to be moved. Eventually they gathered around the open grave. Though the morning was pleasant, Pip was shivering violently. Robin knew he felt as though he would never be warm again. She moved to comfort him, but Jack had already thrown her arms around him.

Robin quickly took her place beside Sam, reaching for his hand, praying that he would not feel abandoned. But Sam's face was peaceful; he beamed at his wife, proudly, and squeezed Robin's hand. The sunlight caught a small gold pin on the lapel of his suit. Robin had never noticed it before. She was surprised to see that it was a beautiful depiction of Saint Joseph, tenderly cradling his Foster Child.

One by one, they said their silent good-byes to Johnathon, and each sprinkled a handful of freshly turned soil atop his casket. Last of all, Philip dropped a tiny bundle of white violets into the grave.

Turning to leave, Robin caught a glimpse of movement behind their assembled group. Whoever it was had vanished. Sighing deeply, she stooped to retrieve a large feather that had fluttered to the ground. It was a brilliant red feather with gold tips and a marvelous iridescence. "Thank you for coming," she whispered, as she let the feather fall into the grave. It rested next to Pip's violets.

CHAPTER TWENTY-SEVEN

That afternoon, Father George joined the family around the formal dining table for tea. Pip had been up the previous night, as was his habit, preparing the food. Tiny sandwiches of impossibly thin cucumber slices, amazingly light shrimp mousse, and perfectly poached chicken breast. Currant scones and fresh strawberries. All manner of beautiful and delicious pastries. The tea was hot and strong and plentiful.

As Pip poured, he commented on the very first time they had used the lovely tea set. "It was the day that John and I arrived. He thought the cups were so delicate and pretty." No one could quite believe how quickly the months had passed. Or how attached they had become. Or how much they missed their friend.

"Sam and I must be heading home in a few days," Jackson announced. "And we'd like to say, Pip, that we'd love to have you come and live with us."

Pip was stunned—and very touched. He glanced at Robin before replying. "How can I ever thank you for such a generous invitation? And I love you both so dearly. But I thought Robin had told you—I'm staying here!" He grinned the old grin that they had so longed to see these past few weeks.

"It's true," Robin agreed. "We've talked it over. We're going to convert the attic room into a small bedroom and bath."

Jackson was thrilled. "Brilliant! We can come and visit you and Lydia anytime! And always have this mousse!" She reached for another tea sandwich.

Philip and Robin explained that it was all Father George's idea. He suggested that they offer the downstairs suite to couples who came to Fairhope for his blessing.

"It will be perfect!" enthused Philip. "The attic, with its sloped roof and dormer windows, will be adorable! A cozy little nest for me. And this place could use another bathroom. Can't you just see an old cast-iron tub, with ball and claw feet? Nothing fussy, mind you; better to err on the side of…monastic, shall we say? And our guests will at least have a comfortable place to spend the night, and an elegant breakfast the next morning…"

His voice had slowly ground to a stop, as if his attempt at cheerfulness had exhausted him. Everyone knew he had been painting a happy scene for them, being careful to avoid the glaring vacancy in the picture.

Pip covered his face with his hands and started to weep. Wiping at his tears, he appealed to Robin, "Just tell me, how am I supposed to get through this?" They had never heard a more desperate appeal.

Robin looked across the table at her dear sister. Jackson nodded imperceptibly. They both answered Pip, "Father George will tell you."

The kindly priest handed Philip his jacket and led him to the front door. "Let's take a walk, my darling child." Pip obeyed, following his friend and priest out into the evening air. "But where are we going?"

Father George smiled. "To the St. Vitus chapel. There are some people that I'd like you to meet."